How I Saved the World

Bugs Bunny's *Space Jam*™ Scrapbook

by James Preller
Based on the screenplay written by
Leo Benvenuti & Steve Rudnick and Timothy Harris & Herschel Weingrod

SCHOLASTIC INC.
New York Toronto London Auckland Sydney

ISBN 0-590-98480-2

SJSC20

12 11 10 9 8 7 6 5 4 3 2 1 6 7 8 9/9 0 1/0

Designed by Joan Ferrigno

Printed in the U.S.A. 23

First Scholastic printing, November 1996

Eh, what's up, Doc? It's me, Bugs Bunny, movie star and America's favorite Looney Tune. You were expecting maybe the Easter Bunny?

Let me tell you how I saved the world from a big purple bully named Swackhammer.

The Nerdlucks work for Swackhammer.
And people say there's intelligent life in outer space.
I guess they never met Bang, Bupkus, Blanko, Pound, and Nawt.

I not only saved the world. I helped the world's greatest basketball player (besides me, of course) return to the game of basketball. . . .

For awhile, Michael Jordan wanted to be a baseball player. Yeah, right, and Elmer Fudd should become the next president of the United States. You know, that may not be such a bad idea after all. . . .

Then, all this Jordan guy wanted to do was play golf. Now that's an exciting sport. You wear goofy pants. You carry around heavy golf clubs in the hot sun. And you hit a tiny ball into a small hole in the ground.

Doesn't he realize that some perfectly nice little bunnies might be living in those holes?

So there I was, minding my own business, when suddenly these Nerdlucks showed up. They said they wanted to take me for a ride. I laughed. But when they pulled out their ray guns, I went along with the gag.

Swackhammer wanted to kidnap the Looney Tunes and force us to work in his crummy theme park in outer space. Not my idea of a nice summer vacation, you know what I mean.

But I'll admit it. None of us took these little pip-squeaks seriously. Then again, we're Looney Tunes.
We don't take anything seriously.

Yosemite Sam got angry. But he was no match for five tiny aliens with roasty, toasty ray guns.

Here's my feather-headed friend, Daffy Duck — always yapping about something.

Daffy is still mad no one asked him to write a book of his own.

Porky had an idea to challenge the little aliens to a spelling bee.

Elmer Fudd's great idea was to challenge them to a bowling tournament.

No wonder I'm the brains of the organization.

We analyzed the competition:
A small race of invading aliens.
Tiny guys, small arms, short legs.

So we challenged them to a basketball game.
Hey, it seemed like a good idea at the time.

Our first practice didn't go so swell.

You've got to hand it to Foghorn Leghorn.
He's 100 percent chicken.

When Yosemite said he could
shoot the ball . . . well . . .
it wasn't exactly what I had
in mind.

Suddenly, the little pip-squeaks weren't so little anymore. They grew into giant Monstars.

I figured we might
need some help . . .

So I came up with a brilliant idea . . . kidnap Michael Jordan, basketball superstar.

Check out Porky Pig — what a ham! He wants Michael Jordan's autograph. Poor Michael. One minute he's out playing golf, the next minute he's got a pink, pot-bellied pig pushing a pencil in his puss. Besides, if Porky really wanted the signature of the greatest basketball player on the planet . . .

. . . he should have asked me.

The Tune Squad wasn't all bad.
We had Taz, the spinning wonder
from down under.

And of course, Lola, my dream bunny.
She's crazy about me . . . sometimes.
Just don't call
her "doll."

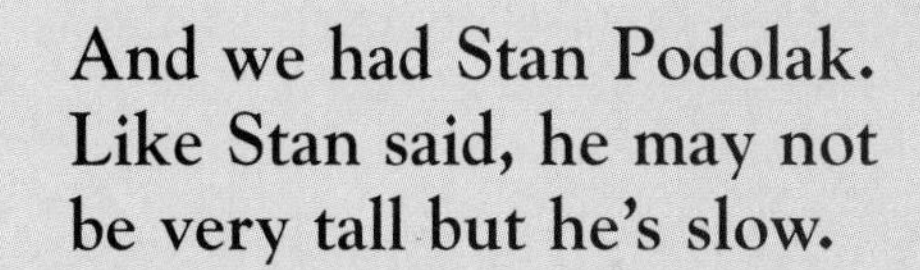
And we had Stan Podolak. Like Stan said, he may not be very tall but he's slow.

Michael Jordan is not the only one who can fly. So can Tweety.

Once the real game started, the Monstars got pretty rough. That heap on the floor is me. What can I say? It was a bad hare day.

The Monstars really messed Stan up at halftime.

Turns out that Jordan guy had not lost his touch . . .

. . . after I gave him
a few pointers.

Geez, what a team. Not a pretty sight, eh?
Things got so bad we even had to let Stan play.
That's plenty bad.

We were getting destroyed at halftime, 64 to 18. So I took a little marker, scribbled down a few words, and changed the course of history.

We played great in the second half. With ten seconds left in the game, we were down by only one point.

So . . .
I decided to be a nice guy
and let that Jordan character
win the game for us.

And that's how I saved the world. It's a big job, but some bunny's got to do it.